P9-DOB-272

HARRIET AND THE PROMISED LAND

JACOB LAWRENCE

HARRIET AND THE PROMISED LAND

Aladdin Paperbacks

To the courageous women of America

With special thanks to Sybille A. Jagusch and the Library of Congress

First Aladdin Paperbacks edition January 1997
Copyright © 1968, 1993 by Jacob Lawrence. First Simon & Schuster edition 1993.

Aladdin Paperbacks
An imprint of Simon & Schuster
Children's Publishing Division
1230 Avenue of the Americas
New York, NY 10020

10 9 8 7

The Library of Congress has cataloged the hardcover edition as follows:
Lawrence, Jacob, 1917- Harriet and the Promised Land/by Jacob Lawrence.   p.   cm.
Summary: A brief biography in verse about Harriet Tubman and her dedicated efforts to
lead her fellow slaves to freedom.   1. Tubman, Harriet. 1815?-1913—Juvenile poetry.
2. Slaves—United States—Biography—Juvenile poetry.   3. Afro-Americans—Biography—
Juvenile poetry.   4. Underground railroad—Juvenile poetry.   5. Children's poetry,
American.   [1. Tubman, Harriet, 1815?-1913—Poetry.   2. Afro-Americans—Poetry.
3. Slaves—Poetry.]   I. Title.   PS3562.A9127H36 1993   811'.54—dc20   92-33740   CIP
ISBN 0-671-86673-7

ISBN 0-689-80965-4 (Aladdin pbk.)

The United States is a great country. It is a great country because of people like John Brown, Frederick Douglass, Abraham Lincoln, Sojourner Truth, and Harriet Tubman.

I recall learning of Harriet Tubman from my mother and from the many schoolteachers and librarians within New York's Harlem community with whom I had the opportunity of coming in contact when I was a very young boy of about five or six years of age. Like so many young people who had this opportunity, I will always remember the drama and the exploits of Harriet.

I was told that Harriet Tubman was born a slave and that she fled her slave masters just prior to the Civil War. She organized other slaves and, moving through the Underground Railroad, made nineteen trips from South to North . . . always following the North Star until she and the other runaway slaves reached the vast, snowy fields of Canada. It was a perilous journey. The slave owners and the hound dogs were always on their tracks, searching for runaway slaves. Harriet Tubman was a very daring and brave woman.

American history has always been one of my favorite subjects. Given the opportunity to select a subject from American history, I chose to do a number of paintings in tribute to Harriet Tubman, a most remarkable woman, and in so doing also to pay tribute and honor to my late mother, Rosalee, and to my wife, Gwen. These three women have contributed much to making it possible for me to develop, to live, to grow, and to fully appreciate the challenges and the beauty of life in general; and to express through the elements of color, line, texture, shape, and value the wisdom of an almighty God.

Jacob Lawrence
October 11, 1992

This is the story of Harriet Tubman, born a slave in Maryland around 1820, who made a daring escape to the North and freedom. At the risk of her life, she returned nineteen times to lead over three hundred of her people to "The Promised Land."

Harriet, Harriet,
Born a slave,

Work for your master

From your cradle
To your grave.

Harriet, clean;
Harriet, sweep.
Harriet, rock
The child to sleep.

Harriet, hear tell
About "The Promised Land":
How Moses led the slaves
Over Egypt's sand,

How Pharaoh's heart
Was hard as stone,
How the Lord told Moses
He was not alone.

Harriet, pray
To the Lord at night
For strength to free your people
When the time is right.

Harriet, grow bigger.
Harriet, grow stronger.
Harriet, work harder.
Harriet, work longer.

Then...
Harriet got the sign
That the time was right.
She cried, "Brothers! Sisters!
I'll lead you tonight!"

The North Star shone
To light Harriet's way;
And they marched by night,
And they slept by day.

Some were afraid,
But none turned back,
For close at their heels
Howled the bloodhound pack.

A snake said, *"Hiss!"*
An owl said, *"Whoo!"*
Harriet said, "We are
Coming through!"

A runaway slave
With a price on her head,
"I'll be free," said Harriet,
"Or I'll be dead!"

She said, "Believe in the Lord!"
She said, "Believe in me!"
She said, "Brothers! Sisters!
We're going to be free!"

They slept in a barn
With the barnyard fowl.
And Harriet kept watch
Like a barnyard owl.

Good people gave
Them food to eat
And a chance to rest
Their weary feet.

They gave Harriet chickens
To disguise
The runaway slave
From spying eyes.

Then the north wind howled
Like a bloodhound pack;
But none were afraid,
And none turned back.

Harriet led them 'cross the snow
Toward "The Promised Land,"
As Moses led his people
'Cross the burning sand.

They marched through the cold,
They marched through the heat;
And the only sound
Was their marching feet.
Now they marched by day,
Now they marched by night;
Still "The Promised Land"
Was not in sight.
Now Harriet grew weary
And sick at heart.
Now the Lord
Sent Harriet
A chariot!

The chariot was sent
By the Lord's own hand,
And Harriet
Rode the chariot
To "The Promised Land!"

Harriet, Harriet,
Born to be free,
Led her people
To liberty!